This book belongs to

....

For my mum and dad and sister, Mandi,
who always believed in me. And for Dave,
who made me believe in myself.

Goose
Copyright © 2012 by Laura Wall
All rights reserved. Manufactured in China.

www.harpercollinschildrens.com

ISBN 978-0-06-232435-1 (trade bdg.)

The artwork for this book was drawn with charcoal and finished digitally.

14 15 16 17 18 SCP 10 9 8 7 6 5 4 3 2 1

First U.S. edition, 2015

Originally published in the U.K. by Award Publications Limited

Goose

by Laura Wall

HARPER

An Imprint of HarperCollinsPublishers

This is Sophie.

She likes to play with her dolls.

And dress up.

But this isn't much fun by herself.

Sophie's mom takes her to the park.

Sophie wants to go on the seesaw.

But someone else is already on it.

So instead she sits on the slide.

And swings on the swings.

Sophie wishes she had a
friend to play with.

But wait. What's that?

A
goose!

The goose follows Sophie.

They play on the seesaw.

And on the slide.

And they swing on the swings.

When it is time to go home,
Goose wants to come, too.

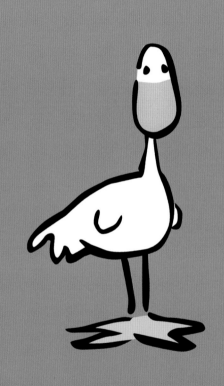

But Mom says no.

"Good-bye, Goose!"

The next day Sophie goes back to the park.

And who should be there but Goose!

They play on the seesaw again.

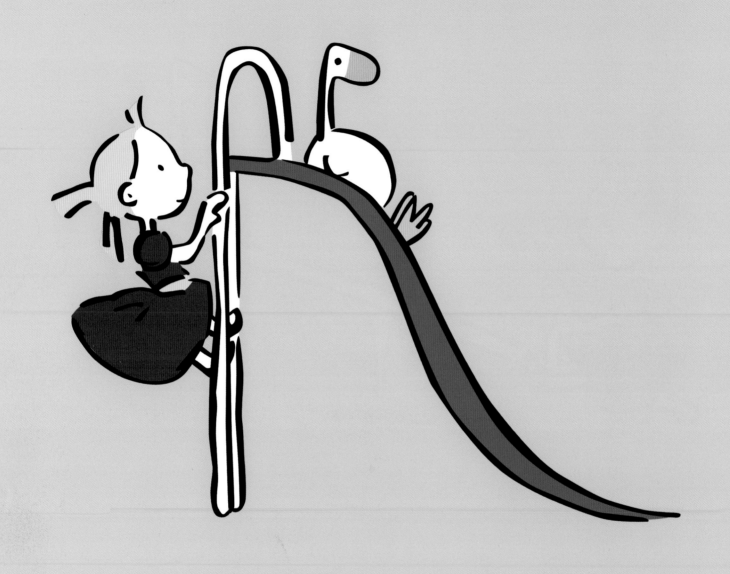

And on the slide.

And they swing on the swings.

Then Goose looks sad.

His friends are flying away for the winter.
It is time for him to go.

"Good-bye, Goose!"

The next day Sophie goes to the park again.

But Goose is not there.

Nothing is quite as much fun.

Not without Goose.

But when it is time to go home,
Sophie hears a familiar sound.

Honk!

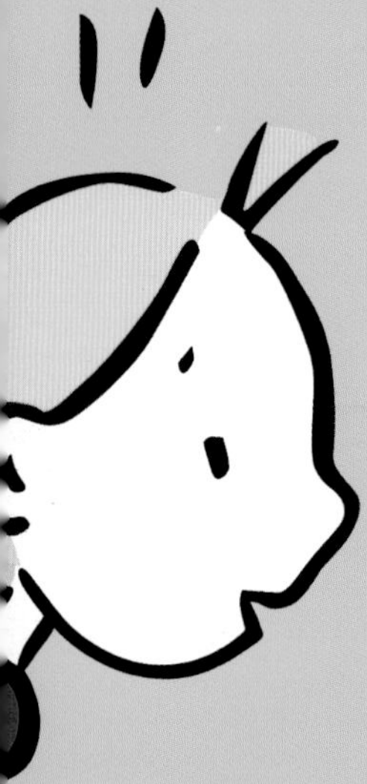

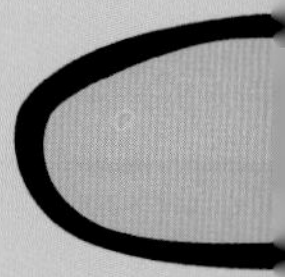

"Goose! You came back!"

"Please can Goose come home?"

"Okay," says Mom.
"If he promises to be good."

"Honk!" says Goose.